GIANT PLANT-EATING DINOSAURS

Consulting Editor: Carl Mehling

Skyview
Books™

an imprint of
WINDMILL BOOKS™
New York

Published in 2010 by Windmill Books, LLC
303 Park Avenue South, Suite # 1280, New York, NY 10010-3657

CREDITS:
Consulting Editor: Carl Mehling
Designer: Graham Beehag

Publisher Cataloging in Publication

Giant plant-eating dinosaurs / consulting editor, Carl Mehling.
    p. cm. – (Discovering dinosaurs)
Summary: With the help of fossil evidence this book provides physical descriptions of thirty-two plant-eating dinosaurs.—Contents: Melanorosaurus—Rhoetosaurus—Omeisaurus—Cetiosaurus—Cetiosauriscus—Bothriospondylus—Dicraeosaurus—Diplodocus—Euhelopus—Haplocanthosaurus—Ultrasauros—Dacentrurus—Brachiosaurus—Seismosaurus—Apatosaurus—Pelorosaurus—Amargasaurus—Argentinosaurus—Aeolosaurus—Alamosaurus—Antarctosaurus—Edmontosaurus—Hypselosaurus—Nemegtosaurus—Neuquensaurus—Opisthocoelicaudia—Quaesitosaurus—Saurolophus—Shantungosaurus—Titanosaurus—Lambeosaurus—Saltasaurus.
ISBN 978-1-60754-778-5. – ISBN 978-1-60754-786-0 (pbk.)
ISBN 978-1-60754-860-7 (6-pack)
1. Dinosaurs—Juvenile literature   2. Herbivores, Fossil—Juvenile literature
[1. Dinosaurs   2. Herbivores, Fossil]   I. Mehling, Carl   II. Series
567.9—dc22

Printed in the United States

CPSIA Compliance Information: Batch #BW10W: For further information contact Windmill Books, New York, New York at 1-866-478-0556.

CONTENTS

4   **Introduction**

5   Melanorosaurus

6   Rhoetosaurus

7   Omeisaurus

8   Cetiosaurus

9   Cetiosauriscus

10   Bothriospondylus

11   Dicraeosaurus

12   Diplodocus

13   Euhelopus

14   Haplocanthosaurus

15   Ultrasauros

16   Dacentrurus

18   Brachiosaurus

22   Seismosaurus

24   Apatosaurus

25   Pelorosaurus

26   Amargasaurus

30   Argentinosaurus

31   Aeolosaurus

32   Alamosaurus

33   Antarctosaurus

34   Edmontosaurus

35   Hypselosaurus

36   Nemegtosaurus

37   Neuquensaurus

38   Opisthocoelicaudia

39   Quaesitosaurus

40   Saurolophus

41   Shantungosaurus

42   Titanosaurus

43   Lambeosaurus

44   Saltasaurus

45   **Glossary**

46   **Index**

48   **For More Information**

Introduction

Imagining what our world was like in the distant past is a lot like being a detective. There were no cameras around, and there were no humans writing history books. In many cases, fossils are all that remain of animals who have been extinct for millions of years.

Fossils are the starting point that scientists use to make educated guesses about what life was like in prehistoric times. And while fossils are important, even the best fossil can't tell the whole story. If snakes were extinct, and all we had left were their bones, would anyone guess that they could snatch bats from the air in pitch-black caves? Probably not, but there is a Cuban species of snake that can do just that. Looking at a human skeleton wouldn't tell you how many friends that person had, or what their favorite color was. Likewise, fossils can give us an idea of how an animal moved and what kind of food it ate, but they can't tell us everything about an animal's behavior or what life was like for them.

Our knowledge of prehistoric life is constantly changing to fit the new evidence we have. While we may never know everything, the important thing is that we continue to learn and discover. Learning about the history of life on Earth, and trying to piece together the puzzle of the dinosaurs, can help us understand more about our past and future.

Melanorosaurus

• **ORDER** • Saurischia • **FAMILY** • Melanorosauridae • **GENUS & SPECIES** • *Melanorosaurus readi, M. thabanensis*

VITAL STATISTICS

FOSSIL LOCATION	South Africa
DIET	Herbivorous
PRONUNCIATION	MEH-luh-nor-oh-SAW-rus
WEIGHT	Unknown
LENGTH	39 ft (12 m)
HEIGHT	14 ft (4.3 m)
MEANING OF NAME	"Black Mountain lizard" after the location of the site where it was found

FOSSIL EVIDENCE

The hips have four sacral vertebrae, and the thigh bone is straight. These features allowed the animal to carry its huge weight on all four pillar-like legs, and it probably could not walk on its hind legs. However, its back legs were still longer than its front legs. The spinal bones had hollow spaces to reduce their weight. So far no head has been found, but sauropod teeth were not designed for chewing so they may have swallowed stones to aid digestion. It had a long neck and tail.

This giant herbivore probably moved on four legs instead of two because of its size and weight. It was one of the largest early dinosaurs.

DIGESTING FOOD

One way large herbivorous dinosaurs may have digested large amounts of plant matter was to swallow stones that would grind up the contents of the stomach. These stones are called gastroliths.

WHERE IN THE WORLD?

Found on the Thaba 'Nyama (Black Mountain) in Transkei, South Africa.

HOW BIG IS IT?

CLAWED THUMB

Like all prosauropods, *Melanorosaurus* had small fingers and a large clawed thumb. This may have been using for digging out food and for defense.

DINOSAUR

TRIASSIC

TIMELINE (millions of years ago)

540	505	438	408	360	280	248	208	146	65	1.8 to today

Rhoetosaurus

• **ORDER** • Saurischia • **FAMILY** • Incertae cedis • **GENUS & SPECIES** • *Rhoetosaurus brownei*

VITAL STATISTICS

FOSSIL LOCATION	Australia
DIET	Herbivorous
PRONUNCIATION	REET-oh-SAWR-us
WEIGHT	Unknown
LENGTH	39-56 ft (12-17 m)
HEIGHT	16 ft (5 m)
MEANING OF NAME	"Rhoetan lizard" after the giant Rhoetus of Greek mythology

WHERE IN THE WORLD?

So many dinosaur bones have been found in one area of Queensland that it's nicknamed the "fossil triangle."

Rhoetosaurus is one of Australia's largest sauropods and one of the world's earliest known sauropods. Although its exact weight is unknown, *Rhoetosaurus* may have weighed as much as four elephants.

FOSSIL EVIDENCE

Discovered in stages, the first pieces of *Rhoetosaurus* were uncovered by a station manager named Arthur Browne near Roma, in Queensland, in 1924. When those pieces were found to be vertebrae of a new species, an expedition set out to find more of the *Rhoetosaurus* fossil. In 1926, parts of *Rhoetosaurus*'s tail, neck, ribs and hind leg were found. More remains were discovered in 1975. The massive weight of this sauropod was supported by column-like legs that had a femur an impressive 5 ft (1.5 m) long.

SPINE
Light-weight vertebrae with cartilage at the center made *Rhoetosaurus*'s spine weigh less and made it more flexible than solid bone.

REAR FOOT
Possibly designed for hauling bulky *Rhoetosaurus* up slopes, the rear feet had a large claw on the first toe that dug into the ground for traction.

HOW BIG IS IT?

DINOSAUR

JURASSIC

TIMELINE (millions of years ago)

540	505	438	408	360	280	248	208	146	65	1.8 to today

Omeisaurus

• **ORDER** • Saurischia • **FAMILY** • Unranked • **GENUS & SPECIES** • *Omeisaurus junghsiensis*

VITAL STATISTICS

FOSSIL LOCATION	China
DIET	Herbivorous
PRONUNCIATION	OH-may-SAWR-us
WEIGHT	unknown
LENGTH	59-66 ft (18-20 m)
HEIGHT	30 ft (9 m)
MEANING OF NAME	"Omei lizard" after China's Mount Omei near the fossil's location

WHERE IN THE WORLD?

Located in Szechuan, Mount Omei is one of the four Buddhist mountains of China that are considered sacred.

Like a typical sauropod, *Omeisaurus* had four column-like legs and ate plants. It did have the unusual trait of having nostrils closer to the end of its snout than other sauropods.

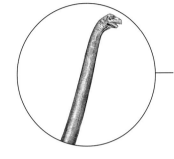

NECK
Omeisaurus had more neck vertebrae than most other sauropods. These vertebrae were also longer and stronger than in most other sauropods.

FOSSIL EVIDENCE

Its amazingly long neck allowed *Omeisaurus* to feed on leaves at the tops of tall trees. However, it also meant that *Omeisaurus*' head was carried far above its heart. With at least three more neck vertebrae than the average sauropod, *Omeisaurus* needed a heavy, powerful heart to pump blood the long distance to its brain. Wide, muscular arteries in the neck carried blood at an extremely high pressure. Valves in the arteries prevented too much blood from rushing to *Omeisaurus*'s brain when it bent its neck downward.

HOW BIG IS IT?

TAIL
Omeisaurus is usually shown with a clubbed tail, but paleontologists argue that the club actually belonged to a *Shunosaurus* that died nearby.

DINOSAUR

MID JURASSIC

TIMELINE (millions of years ago)

540	505	438	408	360	280	248	208	146	65	1.8 to today

Cetiosaurus

• ORDER • Saurischia • FAMILY • Cetiosauridae • GENUS & SPECIES • *Cetiosaurus oxoniensi.*

VITAL STATISTICS

FOSSIL LOCATION	England
DIET	Herbivorous
PRONUNCIATION	SEE-tee-oh-SAWR-us
WEIGHT	9 tons (9.9 tonnes)
LENGTH	49-60 ft (15-18 m)
HEIGHT	16 ft (9 m)
MEANING OF NAME	"Whale lizard" because its vertebrae had a size and structure similar to a whale's

FOSSIL EVIDENCE

Cetiosaurus was discovered in 1841, but was not recognized as a dinosaur until 1869. At the time it was first studied, *Cetiosaurus* was the largest land animal scientists had ever seen. Its fossil was first thought to be some sort of marine reptile. *Cetiosaurus* was actually a herbivore that walked slowly on four enormous, pillar-like legs, stripping the countryside of foliage with its peg-like teeth.

WHERE IN THE WORLD?

The northern coast of England's Isle of Wight has yielded a wide variety of fossils, including *Cetiosaurus*.

Cetiosaurus was the first sauropod to be discovered and described. *Cetiosaurus* had heavy backbones (vertebrae) so it usually held its neck straight out from its body instead of raising its head.

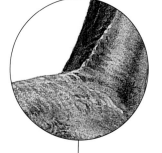

SPINE
Its heavy vertebrae were massive and primitive, unlike the light-weight, hollowed-out bones of later sauropods. This made its long neck less flexible.

HOW BIG IS IT?

BACK LEG
With a thigh bone measuring 6 ft (1.8 m,) *Cetiosaurus* had enormous legs.

DINOSAUR

MID- LATE JURASSIC

TIMELINE (millions of years ago)

540	505	438	408	360	280	248	208	146	65	1.8 to today

Cetiosauriscus

• **ORDER** • Saurischia • **FAMILY** • Diplodocidae • **GENUS & SPECIES** • *Cetiosauriscus stewartensi*

VITAL STATISTICS

FOSSIL LOCATION	England
DIET	Herbivorous
PRONUNCIATION	SEE-tee-oh-sawr-ISS-kus
WEIGHT	Unknown
LENGTH	49 ft (15 m)
HEIGHT	20 ft (6 m)
MEANING OF NAME	"Whale-lizard-like" because it looked similar to *Cetiosaurus*

Cetiosauriscus turned out to be more closely related to *Diplodocus* than *Cetiosaurus*, who it was named after. A lumbering sauropod, *Cetiosauriscus* swallowed leaves whole, possibly relying on gastroliths in its gizzard to crush the food.

WHERE IN THE WORLD?

As the pounding sea erodes the cliffs of England's southern coastline, new fossils are slowly exposed, including those of *Cetiosauriscus*.

TEETH
Cetiosauriscus cropped plants with the peg-like teeth in the front of its mouth. It swallowed plants whole without chewing them.

TAIL
Cetiosauriscus may have flicked its tail, which narrowed at the end, to produce loud cracking noises when competing for female attention or frightening enemies.

FOSSIL EVIDENCE

Cetiosauriscus could not lift its head much higher than its shoulders, so it grazed on lower-lying vegetation. Its long neck poked into thick foliage or reached plants growing on ground that was too marshy to support its massive weight. From the base of the tail to its tip, the vertebrae of *Cetiosauriscus* got smaller, giving the tail a tapering appearance. A series of forked bones in the tail possibly protected the blood vessels if *Cetiosauriscus* was able to stand on its hind legs, using the tail as a prop.

HOW BIG IS IT?

DINOSAUR

MID- LATE JURASSIC

TIMELINE (millions of years ago)

540	505	438	408	360	280	248	208	146	65	1.8 to today

Bothriospondylus

• **ORDER** • Saurischia • **FAMILY** • Brachiosauridae • **GENUS & SPECIES** • *Bothriospondylus robustus*

VITAL STATISTICS

FOSSIL LOCATION	Madagascar, England, Tanzania
DIET	Herbivorous
PRONUNCIATION	BAWTH-ree-oh-SPON-di-lus
WEIGHT	Unknown
LENGTH	66 ft (20 m)
HEIGHT	35 ft (10.7 m)
MEANING OF NAME	"Furrowed vertebrae" because of the shape of its vertebrae

WHERE IN THE WORLD?

England, Madagascar and Tanzania.

NOSTRILS
Nostrils placed on top of its head allowed *Bothriospondylus* to breathe while eating without inhaling little pieces of plant material.

When *Bothriospondylus* fossils were first discovered, scientists had a hard time imagining such an huge creature walking on land all the time without getting tired. Experts originally thought it lived part of its life in water.

FOSSIL EVIDENCE

Bothriospondylus had longer front legs than back legs, which helped support the weight of its incredibly long neck. Its long neck gave it the reach it needed to graze the tops of trees, where its spoon-shaped teeth tore off leaves. Instead of chewing the leaves to a pulp, *Bothriospondylus* swallowed them in a shredded form. Gastroliths (swallowed stones) that it probably had in its gizzard did the work of grinding the plant material into a digestible form.

TEETH
Long, spoon-shaped teeth helped *Bothriospondylus* tear off coarse leaves from high trees. It used these teeth to shred rather than chew.

HOW BIG IS IT?

DINOSAUR

LATE JURASSIC

TIMELINE (millions of years ago)

540	505	438	408	360	280	248	208	146	65	1.8 to today

Dicraeosaurus

• ORDER • Saurischia • FAMILY • Dicraeosauridae • GENUS & SPECIES • *Dicraeosaurus hansemanni*

VITAL STATISTICS

FOSSIL LOCATION	Tanzania
DIET	Herbivorous
PRONUNCIATION	Die-CREE-oh-SAWR-us
WEIGHT	15 tons (16.5 tonnes)
LENGTH	43-66 ft (13-20 m)
HEIGHT	20 ft (6 m)
MEANING OF NAME	"Forked lizard" after the forked spines on its vertebrae

FOSSIL EVIDENCE

Dicraeosaurus was a large sauropod that lived during the Late Jurassic. It lived near other herbivores that probably fed on different types of plants at different heights, so they were not competing for the same vegetation. Once it had cleared an area of the plants it liked, *Dicraeosaurus* moved on to a new area. *Dicraeosaurus* may have traveled in herds, with the dominant adults leading the way, the young following closely behind, and the elderly bringing up the rear. The adults may have surrounded the young for protection when under attack.

DINOSAUR

LATE JURASSIC

WHERE IN THE WORLD?

Dicraeosaurus bones were discovered in the Tendaguru beds of Tanzania, a fossil-rich site.

As a herbivore, *Dicraeosaurus* did not have many defenses against predators. However, a sauropod of its size could rely on its size alone as a deterrent against attack.

TEETH
Dicraeosaurus had blunt teeth like other sauropods. These teeth were suited for stripping the huge amount of vegetation it ate daily.

HOW BIG IS IT?

LEGS
Bulky *Dicraeosaurus* was not very fast. It probably plodded slowly on the four pillar-like legs that supported its hefty body.

TIMELINE (millions of years ago)

540	505	438	408	360	280	248	208	146	65	1.8 to today

Diplodocus

• **ORDER** • Saurischia • **FAMILY** • Diplodocidae • **GENUS & SPECIES** • *Diplodocus longu*...

VITAL STATISTICS

FOSSIL LOCATION	Western US
DIET	Herbivorous
PRONUNCIATION	Di-PLOD-oh-kus
WEIGHT	10-20 tons (11-22 tonnes)
LENGTH	90 ft (27 m)
HEIGHT	16 ft (5 m) at the hips
MEANING OF NAME	"Double-beamed" because of the structure of the bones in the underside of its tail

FOSSIL EVIDENCE

At first, nostrils on top of its skull led scientists to believe that *Diplodocus* lived in water. They imagined that *Diplodocus* would submerge itself in water up to the top of its head and use the nostrils as a snorkeling device to breathe. The placement of the nostrils may have actually allowed *Diplodocus* to breathe while eating without inhaling tiny bits of stripped foliage. Like other sauropods, *Diplodocus* spent its days grazing on tender leaves. Fossilized skin impressions indicate *Diplodocus* had small spines along its back.

DINOSAUR

LATE JURASSIC

WHERE IN THE WORLD?

Wyoming's Morrison Formation contains many fossils dating to the Jurassic rivers and floodplains.

TAIL
Diplodocus held its whiplash tail above the ground rather than dragging it along the ground. The enormous tail counterbalanced its huge neck.

HOW BIG IS IT?

Diplodocus is the longest dinosaur known from a complete skeleton. Its neck measured 26 ft (8 m) long and contained 15 vertebrae. Its tail stretched 45 ft (14 m) long and was made up of almost 80 vertebrae.

BELLY RIBS
A series of belly "ribs," or gastralia, stretched across *Diplodocus*'s underside and protected its internal organs. These "ribs" were buried in the muscles of the belly.

TIMELINE (millions of years ago)

540	505	438	408	360	280	248	208	146	65	1.8 to today

Euhelopus

• ORDER • Saurischia **• FAMILY •** Euhelopodidae **• GENUS & SPECIES •** *Euhelopus zdanski*

VITAL STATISTICS

FOSSIL LOCATION	China
DIET	Herbivorous
PRONUNCIATION	You-HEL-oh-pus
WEIGHT	Unknown
LENGTH	33-49 ft (10-15 m)
HEIGHT	16 ft (5 m)
MEANING OF NAME	"Good marsh foot" because its broad hind feet were thought to be perfect for walking on marshy ground

FOSSIL EVIDENCE

The theory that *Euhelopus* spent any part of its life submerged in water has been disproved by carefully studying the dinosaur's body. The water pressure against the chest of a creature the size of *Euhelopus* would have been too great for the animal to breathe. *Euhelopus*, like many other sauropods, could not raise its head much above the level of its shoulders.

The nostrils on the top of *Euhelopus*'s head are similar to those of swimming creatures. Scientists first thought that Euhelopus lived submerged underwater, poking only the top of its head out of water to breathe.

NECK
Euhelopus's long, flexible neck could stretch far between trees or over a lake's surface possibly to reach aquatic plants.

WHERE IN THE WORLD?

China's Shandong Province, where *Euhelopus* was discovered, lies to the east of the majestic Taihang Mountains.

FEET
Euhelopus walked on four stout legs. Its broad feet spread its weight over a wide area, which stopped it from sinking into soft soil.

HOW BIG IS IT?

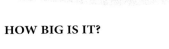

DINOSAUR
LATE JURASSIC

TIMELINE (millions of years ago)

540	505	438	408	360	280	248	208	146	65	1.8 to today

13

Haplocanthosaurus

ORDER • Saurischia • **FAMILY** • Camarasauridae • **GENUS & SPECIES** • *Haplocanthosaurus priscu...*

VITAL STATISTICS

FOSSIL LOCATION	Western US
DIET	Herbivorous
PRONUNCIATION	Hap-lo-KAN-tho-SAWR-us
WEIGHT	13 tons (14.3 tonnes)
LENGTH	71 ft (21.5 m)
HEIGHT	23 ft (7 m)
MEANING OF NAME	"Single-spine lizard" because of the simplicity of its vertebrae

The most primitive sauropod found in North America, *Haplocanthosaurus* had a shorter neck and tail than other sauropods. Slow-moving *Haplocanthosaurus* possibly moved in herds, always looking for a fresh supply of plants.

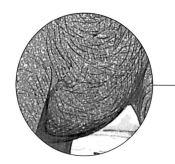

GUT
Because its diet of cycads and conifers was low in nutrients, *Haplocanthosaurus* had to eat massive amounts of plant material for energy.

WHERE IN THE WORLD?

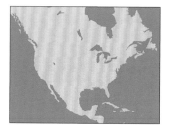

Haplocanthosaurus was first discovered by a college student who was digging in Colorado's Morrison Formation.

FOSSIL EVIDENCE

Fossilized tracks prove that sauropods like *Haplocanthosaurus* did not drag their tails along the ground. The lack of the drag mark the tail would have made indicates that it was held above the ground to balance the dinosaur's long neck. A giant sauropod the size of *Haplocanthosaurus* could potentially leave a footprint in soft soil that was over 3.2 ft (1 m) long and as deep as 18 in (0.5 m). Its rear feet made larger tracks than its front feet.

NECK
The bones in *Haplocanthosaurus'* shoulder and neck were almost solid. This may have made it difficult for it to lift its head above its shoulders.

HOW BIG IS IT?

DINOSAUR

LATE JURASSIC

TIMELINE (millions of years ago)

540	505	438	408	360	280	248	208	146	65	1.8 to today

Ultrasauros

ORDER • Saurischia • **FAMILY** • Incertae sedis • **GENUS & SPECIES** • *Ultrasauros macintoshi*

VITAL STATISTICS

FOSSIL LOCATION	Western USA
DIET	Herbivorous
PRONUNCIATION	UL-trah-SAWR-ohs
WEIGHT	55-130 tons (60.6-143.3 tonnes)
LENGTH	82-98 ft (25-30 m)
HEIGHT	49-52 ft (15-16 m)
MEANING OF NAME	"Ultra lizard" after its gigantic size

FOSSIL EVIDENCE

Ultrasauros was so huge even a *Ceratosaurus* or *Allosaurus* might be afraid to attack it. A herd of these enormous sauropods would be too intimidating to approach. Moving slowly from tree to tree, *Ultrasauros* walked on four pillar-like legs. If these animals lived in herds, the ground may have trembled under their feet. Many scientists think that *Ultrasauros* may just be a large kind of *Brachiosaurus*.

If it didn't die from disease, an accident or a pack of hungry predators, gigantic *Ultrasauros* may have lived for up to 100 years.

BRAIN
A dinosaur's intelligence is estimated by comparing its body size to its brain size. *Ultrasauros'* tiny head contained a small brain.

NECK
Like other sauropods *Ultrasauros* probably could not raise its head, much like a giraffe.

HOW BIG IS IT?

WHERE IN THE WORLD?

Colorado, where the majestic Rocky Mountains rise, was home to *Ultrasauros* during the late Jurassic period.

DINOSAUR

LATE JURASSIC

TIMELINE (millions of years ago)

540	505	438	408	360	280	248	208	146	65	1.8 to today

Dacentrurus

VITAL STATISTICS

FOSSIL LOCATION	Europe
DIET	Herbivorous
PRONUNCIATION	Dah-sen-TROO-rus
WEIGHT	1–2 tons (1–2 tonnes)
LENGTH	Up to 33 ft (10 m)
HEIGHT	Unknown
MEANING OF NAME	"Very sharp tail" because of its long spikes

Deciding what a dinosaur looked like from a jumbled and incomplete skeleton can be very hard. Especially when some of the bones may not even be from that animal! The story of how we learned about *Dacentrurus* took many twists and turns. First it was named *Omasaurus*, but then scientists realized another dinosaur had already been given that name. Then its estimated size began to balloon. Sometimes listed as being 15 ft (4.4 m) long, it is now thought to be the largest of the stegosaurs at perhaps 33 ft (10 m) in length— rivaling its more famous relative *Stegosaurus*.

WHERE IN THE WORLD?

Remains found in England, France, Spain and the Louriñha site in Portugal.

FOSSIL EVIDENCE

This was the first of the stegosaurs to be named, in 1875 in England. It was also found in France and Spain in the 1990s and, most usefully, in Portugal. Here, five complete juvenile skeletons have been discovered, as well as an egg that may have belonged to the species. The French fossils were destroyed during World War II when the Le Havre museum where they were stored was bombed. The features of the specimens studied are so different that some argue they are from different species.

TAIL SPIKES
This was an ambling plant-eater that may have relied on its sharp tail spikes to protect it from faster predators.

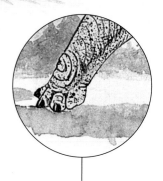

TOES
Dacentrurus had three toes on each foot and four fingers on each hand, like other members of its family. Because it didn't have claws, we know it must have depended on its armor for defense.

HOW BIG IS IT?

DINOSAUR

LATE JURASSIC

ORDER • Ornithischia • **FAMILY** • Stegosauridae • **GENUS & SPECIES** • *Dacentrurus armatus*

BIGGER THAN FIRST THOUGHT

The largest pelvis discovered measures 5 ft (1.5 m) across, which is why some paleontologists argue that the size of this beast is actually much larger than we thought. An animal whose hips are that far apart is going to be very big, especially when you consider that some femurs measure more than 3 ft (1 m). Part of the difficulty in agreeing on its size is that the more complete smaller specimens are juveniles.

BACK PLATES

The bone plates on its back are shaped more like spikes than triangles, which lets us know that it is an early stegosaurid. The plates are positioned in two rows along the back, with a double row of long, sharp-edged spikes on the lower back and tail. The longest spike found is 18 in (45 cm) to the tip. The plates and spines are arranged very differently from how they were on *Stegosaurus*.

FORELIMBS AND VERTEBRAE
The long forelimbs and primitive vertebrae are more evidence that this is a very early stegosaurid.

TIMELINE (millions of years ago)

540	505	438	408	360	280	248	208	146	65	1.8 to today

Brachiosaurus

VITAL STATISTICS

Fossil Location	US, Europe, Africa
Diet	Herbivorous
Pronunciation	BRACK-ee-uh-SAWR-us
Weight	35-41 tons (32-37 tonnes)
Length	82 ft (25 m)
Height	42 ft (13 m)
Meaning of name	"Arm reptile" because of its long forelimbs

FOSSIL EVIDENCE

Estimates of the size and weight of *Brachiosaurus* vary wildly. The eyes and nostrils were set high on its head. The large nasal openings near the snout suggest *Brachiosaurus* had a good sense of smell. It was not able to chew, and food was probably digested with the help of stones held in the gizzard, like chickens do today.

We used to think *Brachiosaurus* was a lot like a giraffe—a massive plant-eater that could stretch its long neck to reach the highest leaves. Many scientists now believe that it couldn't hold its neck vertically. Brachiosaurs are some of the largest and heaviest land animals ever; their huge size and leathery skin was probably protection enough from the Late Jurassic carnivores such as *Allosaurus*. The amount of fuel needed to keep such a giant going has added to the discussion about whether some dinosaurs were warm-blooded. If it generated its own heat, *Brachiosaurus* would have needed to eat 440 lb (220 kg) of leaf matter a day. A cold-blooded animal would have needed less.

SKULL AND NECK
The skull had many hollows to restrict its weight. Lifting a solid skull on such a long neck would have been impossible.

FORELEGS
Brachiosaurus takes its name from its extended forelegs. The thigh bone alone was 6.5 ft (2 m) in length.

TEETH
Brachiosaurus teeth were spatulate, like peg-shaped chisels, able to nip off fresh shoots at the top of trees. There were 26 each on the top and bottom jaws.

HOW BIG IS IT?

DINOSAUR

LATE JURASSIC

ORDER • Saurischia • **FAMILY** • Brachiosauridae • **GENUS & SPECIES** • *Brachisaurus altihorax, B. brancai*

USES FOR A LONG NECK

The 14 vertebrae of the long, upright neck have hollow spaces in them—otherwise it would have been too heavy to lift. Early paleontologists thought the animal could have lived underwater, using its neck to keep the nostrils sucking in air above the waves like a snorkel. While the water would have supported its huge body, the pressure would have collapsed its lungs, and the soft mud would not have provided enough support for its narrow feet to stop the animal from sinking. The neck may also have been used in battles for dominance between rival males.

CARDIOVASCULAR POWER

An animal of this size needed an incredibly powerful heart to pump blood along the long distance of the neck to the brain. It would have had muscular blood vessels with many valves to prevent blood flowing backward, and its blood pressure was probably three or four times as high as ours.

WHERE IN THE WORLD?

After the first discovery in western Colorado, there have been finds in southern Europe and northern Africa.

TIMELINE (millions of years ago)

| 540 | 505 | 438 | 408 | 360 | 280 | 248 | 208 | 146 | 65 | 1.8 to today |

Brachiosaurus

ORDER • Saurischia • **FAMILY** • Brachiosauridae • **GENUS & SPECIES** • *Brachiosaurus altihorax, B. brancai*

ONE OF THE LARGEST JURASSIC DINOSAURS

Brachiosaurus, one of the largest dinosaurs of the Jurassic Period, lived around the same time as *Stegosaurus, Dryosaurus, Apatosaurus* and *Diplodocus*, none of which was exactly small. In fact, *Apatosaurus* was slightly bigger than *Brachiosaurus*, while *Diplodocus*—up to 147 ft (45 m) long—was a massive 56 percent bigger. Huge dinosaurs like these made gigantic demands on their environment and also needed a body powerful enough to keep them alive and active. The land they lived on had a lot of food, like ferns, bennettites and horsetails, and they also probably relied on the groves of cycads and ginkgos that grew in the forests. Yet *Brachiosaurus* alone probably needed 401 lb (182 kg) of food every day. Some paleontologists think that they moved around in herds, so the amount of food they all took each day from their environment would have been huge. But their enormous size did, at least, give *Brachiosaurus* important advantages. Some paleontologists believe that *Brachiosaurus* and other large dinosaurs were gigantotherms. This means that the ratio between their volume and their surface area allowed them to keep their body temperature high. Also, with more of their body shielded from close contact with the outside, they lost less body heat to their environment.

Seismosaurus

VITAL STATISTICS

FOSSIL LOCATION	United States
DIET	Herbivorous
PRONUNCIATION	SIZE-moe-SAWR-us
WEIGHT	Up to 55 tons (50 tonnes)
LENGTH	Up to 148 ft (45 m)
HEIGHT	Up to 43 ft (13 m)
MEANING OF NAME	"Earthquake reptile" because it could have made the ground shake

FOSSIL EVIDENCE

Seismosaurus was named in 1991 from a set of bones that included several vertebrae and other spine parts, some ribs and part of the pelvis. With these fossils were many probable gastroliths: stones swallowed by the animal to possibly grind down the food in its gizzard. The model of the animal that scientists built is longer than the *Diplodocus* it looks so much like, but it is thought to have lived the same tree-browsing lifestyle. It was protected by its whip-like tail and its huge size. It was probably simply too big for an enemy to take on.

DINOSAUR

LATE JURASSIC

This was one of the longest land animals that ever walked the Earth. It stomped through the Late Jurassic forests on short legs, swishing its enormous tail and stretching out its extended neck in a constant search for food. As so often in the fossil-studying community, arguments have raged on several points concerning *Seismosarus*. One is whether it could have raised its neck up high as it is often shown doing, given its weight. Another is whether it is a different species from the very similar *Diplodocus* or just an even longer type of that genus.

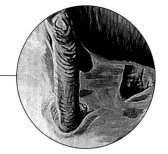

LEGS
Seismosaurus' legs had to be like columns to carry its body. It may have struggled to keep stable on wetlands, preferring firm ground.

TAIL
The tail was very long, and made of about 80 small bones, so it was highly flexible and could possibly have been flung like a whip.

HOW BIG IS IT?

ORDER • Saurischia • **FAMILY** • Diplodocidae • **GENUS & SPECIES** • *Seismosaurus hallorum*

WHERE IN THE WORLD?

The only location for
remains is New Mexico.

TEETH

The teeth look like long pegs, and were used to tear foliage from high branches. Study of wear patterns on the teeth suggests that one row would strip the foliage while the other row guided the direction of the mouth. Food was swallowed without chewing and was digested in the enormous gut, probably with the help of gastroliths.

NECK

The neck was held at a slight upward angle from the ground. It would have been hard for *Seismosaurus* to force its big body through dense woodland, so it probably pushed its neck in at the edges of forests. It may also have lowered its small head toward soft-leaved plants. Some scientists believe it could not have raised its head up very high because of the difficulty in holding up the weight and in keeping blood flowing.

FOSSILS

A fully grown adult collapses and dies. Soon, flying reptiles tear the meat from the body. The rest of the tissue rots away, leaving bones that will be preserved for millions of years.

TIMELINE (millions of years ago)

| 540 | 505 | 438 | 408 | 360 | 280 | 248 | 208 | 146 | 65 | 1.8 to today |

23

Apatosaurus

ORDER • Saurischia • **FAMILY** • Diplodocidae • **GENUS & SPECIES** • *Apatosaurus aja.*

VITAL STATISTICS

FOSSIL LOCATION	Western US, northwestern Mexico
DIET	Herbivorous
PRONUNCIATION	Uh-PAT-uh-SAWR-us
WEIGHT	30 tons (30.5 tonnes)
LENGTH	70–90 ft (21–27 m)
HEIGHT	15 ft (4.6 m) at the hips
MEANING OF NAME	"Deceptive lizard" because some details of its bones were just like those of other mosasaurs

FOSSIL EVIDENCE

In 1879 Othniel Marsh described and named *Brontosaurus* at a time when he was involved in a heated competition called the "bone wars" with his rival Edward Cope. Each man wanted to discover more new dinosaur species than the other. Marsh had a headless specimen of *Apatosaurus* that he was sure was a new species. He gave it a skull based on *Camarasaurus*, which was thought to be a close relative, and with that he invented the *Brontosaurus*. *Apatosaurus* was not reunited with its proper skull until the 1970s. Although *Camarasaurus* and *Apatosaurus* were both sauropods, *Camarasaurus* had a larger skull.

DINOSAUR

LATE JURASSIC

Apatosaurus is one of the most famous dinosaurs ever known. Too bad it became so famous with the wrong name! *Apatosaurus* was given the wrong head and called *Brontosaurus* for almost a hundred years before scientists figured out the mistake.

REAR LEGS
Apatosaurus may have stood on its hind legs to reach high treetops, pressing its tail against the ground to help it balance. Many scientists don't believe that sauropods were built to rear up.

TAIL
Apatosaurus had a whip-like tail that may have cracked loudly when lashed in anger.

WHERE IN THE WORLD?

Wyoming's Nine Mile and Bone Cabin quarries have yielded numerous dinosaur fossils.

HOW BIG IS IT?

TIMELINE (millions of years ago)

540	505	438	408	360	280	248	208	146	65	1.8 to today

Pelorosaurus

• ORDER • Saurischia • FAMILY • Brachiosauridae • GENUS & SPECIES • *Pelorosaurus conybeari*

VITAL STATISTICS

FOSSIL LOCATION	England, Portugal
DIET	Herbivorous
PRONUNCIATION	Pe-LOW-roh-SAWR-us
WEIGHT	Unknown
LENGTH	49–79 ft (15–24 m)
HEIGHT	Unknown
MEANING OF NAME	"Monstrous lizard" after its enormous vertebrae and limb bones

FOSSIL EVIDENCE

Pelorosaurus was identified in the 1840s from several fossil specimens, some of which were later shown to belong to *Iguanodon*. Attempts to reclassify the dinosaur created more confusion, and the identification of later specimens found in Europe may have been wrong too. A specimen found in the Isle of Wight includes vertebrae and pieces of the legs.

WHERE IN THE WORLD?

Some fossils may have been misidentified, so we can only be sure that *Pelorosaurus* lived in England and Portugal.

Against predators, *Pelorosaurus* needed only one defense—its huge body. Its remarkably long neck let it feed high in the foliage, grabbing leaves with its chisel-shaped teeth.

NOSTRILS
Nostrils placed high on top of its head may have helped *Pelorosaurus* avoid inhaling plant material while it ate.

SCALES
Skin impressions left behind with fossils of *Pelorosaurus* show that it was covered in hexagonal scales.

HOW BIG IS IT?

DINOSAUR

EARLY CRETACEOUS

TIMELINE (millions of years ago)

540	505	438	408	360	280	248	208	146	65	1.8 to today

Amargasaurus

VITAL STATISTICS

FOSSIL LOCATION	Argentina
DIET	Herbivorous
PRONUNCIATION	Uh-MARG-uh-SAWR-us
WEIGHT	5.5 tons (5,000 kg)
LENGTH	33 ft (10 m)
HEIGHT	13 ft (4 m)
MEANING OF NAME	"La Amarga lizard" from the canyon where it was found

FOSSIL EVIDENCE

An almost complete skeleton from a single individual was reconstructed and named in 1991. The most interesting feature was the parallel row of tall spines. They are longest at the neck, the tallest reaching 20 in (50 cm), and their height gets smaller as they reach the hips. Neural spines are not unusual in sauropods, but these are the most elaborate by far.

Many mysteries still need to be solved in our quest to understand the world of the dinosaurs, and one is the very interesting question of what *Amargasaurus* really looked like. It was a medium-sized sauropod with the usual features of a bulky body, a long tail and neck and a small head. The mystery lies in the two rows of long spikes running down its back. Were they connected by a thin membrane of skin to form an elaborate double sail, or did they support some sort of fleshy ridge or a colored frill? And what were they for?

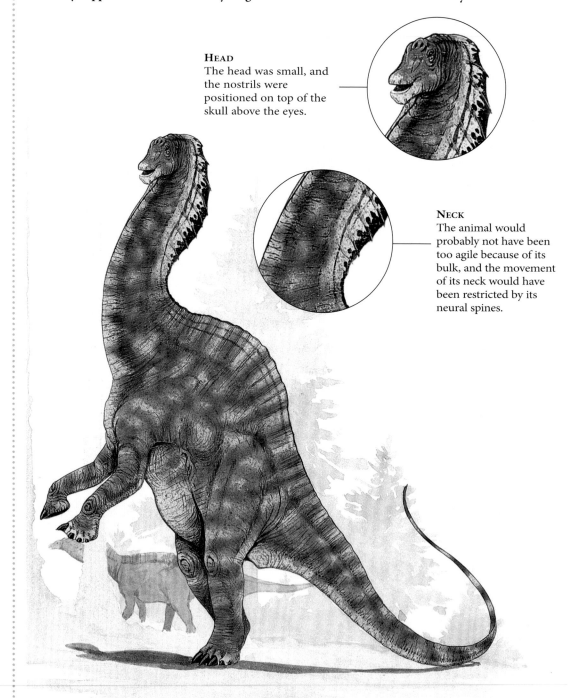

HEAD
The head was small, and the nostrils were positioned on top of the skull above the eyes.

NECK
The animal would probably not have been too agile because of its bulk, and the movement of its neck would have been restricted by its neural spines.

• **ORDER** • Saurischia • **FAMILY** • Dicraeosauridae • **GENUS & SPECIES** • *Amargasaurus cazaui*

A BIGGER APPEARANCE

The most simple explanation for the spines is that they made *Amargasaurus* look bigger. This could have helped to scare off predators and to attract mates during courtship rituals. As a defense measure they weren't much use because the spines were very fragile and would break instead of offering a serious threat to an attacker. As skin-covered sails, they could have been used for thermoregulation, controlling the temperature of the blood, and for display. As a colored mane or frill, it may have changed color to signal to other creatures.

WHERE IN THE WORLD?

The only remains are from the La Armarga canyon in Patagonia in western Argentina.

FEET
Amargasaurus walked on four broad feet, each with five toes, one of them a sharp claw.

HOW BIG IS IT?

TIMELINE (millions of years ago)

| 540 | 505 | 438 | 408 | 360 | 280 | 248 | 208 | 146 | 65 | 1.8 to today |

Amargasaurus

• ORDER • Saurischia **• FAMILY •** Dicraeosauridae **• GENUS & SPECIES •** *Amargasaurus cazaui*

LA AMARGA CREEK DISCOVERY

Models of dinosaurs that we see in museums are not just works of art and imagination, but the result of a lot of research. One good example is a model of *Amargasaurus* discovered at La Amarga Creek, Neuquén Province, in Argentina in 1991. The model went on display in the Melbourne Museum in Victoria, Australia, which opened in 2000. The display shows the the entire skeleton of *Amargasaurus cazaui*, complete with elongated spines along its neck and back. But the *Amargasaurus* skeleton found in Argentina was actually not complete at all—what was found was a portion of the skull, some of the vertebrae with spines, part of the pelvis, and bones from the dinosaur's limbs. With so much missing, the model had to be constructed by using casts of what was there, and filling in the missing parts by using more complete skeletons from other dinosaurs closely related to *Amargasaurus*. One of the relatives used was the enormous herbivore *Diplodocus*, which had similar, though smaller, spines on its back. To be sure that the *Amargasaurus* looked as lifelike as possible, some of the bones had to be remade and scientists studied how the dinosaur would have stood.

Argentinosaurus

• ORDER • Saurischia • FAMILY • unranked • GENUS & SPECIES • *Argentinosaurus huinculensi*

VITAL STATISTICS

FOSSIL LOCATION	South America
DIET	Herbivorous
PRONUNCIATION	Ahr-JEN-oh-SAWR-us
WEIGHT	88 tons (80 tonnes)
LENGTH	115 ft (35 m)
HEIGHT	70 ft (21.4 m)
MEANING OF NAME	"Argentinian lizard" after the country where it was found

This may have been the largest dinosaur that ever lived, but only a few fossils have been found so far. They reveal a giant at the upper limit of how big animals can become and survive.

WHERE IN THE WORLD?

Found in 1987 in the Rio Limay Formation in Neuquén Province, Argentina.

FOSSIL EVIDENCE

From the few bones found, including a 5 ft (1.5 m) shin bone, it is clear this was a massive, long-necked plant eater. One of the vertebrae is 4 ft (1.3 m) long and has a diameter of 5.5 ft (1.7 m). Part of it is wing-shaped, allowing it to hold the powerful muscles needed to hold up the animal. The tail was not as long as that of *Diplodocus*, compared to the size of their bodies. *Argentinosaurus* is thought to have roamed in herds across the wide floodplains of South America that were big enough to provide enough food, and it may have been even bigger than the figures given here.

DINOSAUR

MID CRETACEOUS

SKIN
As a titanosaur, *Argentinosaurus'* skin would have likely been armored with a mosaic of osteoderms, or bony studs.

HEAD LEVEL
Argentinosaurus probably couldn't raise its head much above shoulder height because the blood pressure needed would have burst its veins.

HOW BIG IS IT?

TIMELINE (millions of years ago)

540	505	438	408	360	280	248	208	146	65	1.8 to today

Aeolosaurus

• **ORDER** • Saurischia • **FAMILY** • Titanosauria • **GENUS & SPECIES** • *Aeolosaurus rionegrinus, A. colhuehuapensis*

VITAL STATISTICS

FOSSIL LOCATION	Argentina
DIET	Herbivorous
PRONUNCIATION	EE-oh-loh-SAWR-us
WEIGHT	11 tons (10 tonnes)
LENGTH	49 ft (15 m)
HEIGHT	Unknown
MEANING OF NAME	"Aeolus lizard" after the Greek and Roman god of the winds, because it was found in a windy location

FOSSIL EVIDENCE

Many incomplete skeletons have been discovered showing this was a long-necked, long-tailed quadrupedal plant-eater that may have lived in the swampy lowlands and coastal plains of Argentina. Pieces of armor about 6 in (15 cm) in diameter suggest that its back was at least partially covered by protective plates. A major difference between it and other sauropods is the presence of forward-facing barbs on the tail vertebrae. This implies that *Aeolosaurus* was able to rise on its back legs, propped up by its tail, so that it could reach higher conifer branches.

DINOSAUR

LATE CRETACEOUS

WHERE IN THE WORLD?

Remains come from three separate rock formations in Rio Negro Province, Argentina.

Aeolosaurus was a herbivorous dinosaur that was common in the Southern Hemisphere in the Late Cretacean Period. It roamed in herds, eating large amounts of plant matter to keep its huge body alive.

SMALL TEETH *Aeolosaurus* cropped plant matter off with its small teeth, swallowing it whole since it couldn't chew.

ROBUST LEGS It stood on its four robust, columnar legs most of the time to support its hefty body.

HOW BIG IS IT?

TIMELINE (millions of years ago)

540	505	438	408	360	280	248	208	146	65	1.8 to today

Alamosaurus

• **ORDER** • Saurischia • **FAMILY** • Titanosauridae • **GENUS & SPECIES** • *Alamosaurus sanjuanensis*

VITAL STATISTICS

FOSSIL LOCATION	United States
DIET	Herbivorous
PRONUNCIATION	Al-uh-moe-SAWR-us
WEIGHT	33 tons (30 tonnes)
LENGTH	53 ft (16 m)
HEIGHT	20 ft (6 m)
MEANING OF NAME	"Alamo lizard" after the Ojo Alamo trading post near the first discovery

FOSSIL EVIDENCE

Many pieces of skeleton and bones have been found, showing how widespread and successful *Alamosaurus* became. No skulls have been found yet, and the best specimens are juveniles, from which approximate adult sizes have been estimated. These huge herbivores probably roamed in herds, stripping leaves from tall trees to be digested with the help of gastroliths (swallowed stones) in their gizzards. They survived while sharing territory with predatory tyrannosaurs and other theropods and might have been one of the last non-avian dinosaurs to face extinction.

For many millions of years the record of sauropods in North America is blank. Then *Alamosaurus* appears as fossils in the Late Cretaceous, possibly because its ancestors migrated across a landbridge of the isthmus of Panama from South America and flourished. One estimate suggests there were 350,000 living together in Texas alone.

WHERE IN THE WORLD?

Finds have been uncovered since 1922 in New Mexico, Utah and Texas.

HEIGHT ADVANTAGE
Alamosaurus thrived in the southern United States because it was able to reach the leaves of trees that soared 90 ft (27 m) high in the warm climate.

TAIL
The tail may have worked as a whip to scare off predators. *Alamosaurus* may also have had some body armor.

HOW BIG IS IT?

DINOSAUR

LATE CRETACEOUS

TIMELINE (millions of years ago)

540	505	438	408	360	280	248	208	146	65	1.8 to today

Antarctosaurus

• ORDER • Saurischia • FAMILY • Antarctosauridae • GENUS & SPECIES • *Antarctosaurus wichmannianus*

VITAL STATISTICS

FOSSIL LOCATION	South America and possibly India
DIET	Herbivorous
PRONUNCIATION	Ant-ARK-toe-SAWR-us
WEIGHT	37 tons (34 tonnes)
LENGTH	60 ft (18 m)
HEIGHT	20 ft (6 m)
MEANING OF NAME	"Opposite of north lizard" because it was in the Southern Hemisphere

FOSSIL EVIDENCE

The size of *Antarctosaurus* is not clear. The fossils from the first find were scattered and may not be from the same animal. Some scientists argue about a later find too, which includes a thigh bone measuring 7 ft 9 in (2.35 m). This is double the size of the other and possibly the largest land animal of all time. The figures given here are the lower estimates. This is one of the few sauropods whose skull has been found. It reveals a 2 ft (60 cm) long head with large eyes and a few peg-like teeth at the front of the jaws.

DINOSAUR

LATE CRETACEOUS

This was one of the largest South American sauropods and one of the most widespread dinosaurs in the Southern Hemisphere. It had a large, bulky body supported by tall legs.

TEETH
Antarctosaurus was a plant-eater with a few weak, peg-shaped teeth at the front of the jaws to grab but not chew plant matter.

BODY
The bulky body of this giant probably contained gastroliths (swallowed stones) to crush and grind down the enormous quantities of fibrous greenery it ate.

WHERE IN THE WORLD?

Remains have been found in Argentina and possibly also in India.

HOW BIG IS IT?

Edmontosaurus

• **ORDER** • Ornithischia • **FAMILY** • Hadrosauridae • **GENUS & SPECIES** • *Edmontosaurus regal*

VITAL STATISTICS

FOSSIL LOCATION	Western North America
DIET	Herbivorous
PRONUNCIATION	Ed-MON-toh-SAWR-us
WEIGHT	3.5 tons (3.9 tonnes)
LENGTH	43 ft (13 m)
HEIGHT	Unknown
MEANING OF NAME	"Edmonton lizard" after the Edmonton Rock Formation in Canada, where its fossils were found

Edmontosaurus had a skull like a duck's—flat and broadening out into a beak. Some have suggested that it had loose flaps of skin on its face, which it may have inflated to make bellowing calls.

BEAK
Its beak was toothless, but it had 60 rows of cheek teeth holding about 1000 teeth. It chewed by grinding food against these teeth.

WHERE IN THE WORLD?

Edmontosaurus was found in what is now western North America.

FOSSIL EVIDENCE

Some specimens of *Edmontosaurus* include skin impressions, which show that its skin was scaly and leathery, with tubercles, or tiny bumps, along its neck, down its back and along its tail. Its stomach contents have also been fossilized, showing that it ate the needles, seeds and twigs of conifers. One specimen, displayed at the Denver Museum of Nature and Science, has bite marks at the top of its tail. The only dinosaur large enough to have made such an attack on *Edmontosaurus* is *Tyrannosaurus rex*.

DINOSAUR

LATE CRETACEOUS

HOW BIG IS IT?

FRONT LEGS
Edmontosaurus could probably walk on just two legs, and on all four. Its front limbs had hooves on two digits and weight-bearing pads.

TIMELINE (millions of years ago)

540	505	438	408	360	280	248	208	146	65	1.8 to today

Hypselosaurus

• **ORDER** • Saurischia • **FAMILY** • Titanosauridae • **GENUS & SPECIES** • *Hypselosaurus priscus*

VITAL STATISTICS

FOSSIL LOCATION	France, Spain
DIET	Herbivorous
PRONUNCIATION	HIP-sel-oh-SAWR-us
WEIGHT	9 tons (9.9 tonnes)
LENGTH	39 ft (12 m)
HEIGHT	Unknown
MEANING OF NAME	"High lizard" in reference to its height and long limbs

FOSSIL EVIDENCE

The first non-avian dinosaur eggs ever found probably belonged to *Hypselosaurus*. However, there are some paleontologists who argue that the eggs belong to the flightless bird *Gargantuavis*. The bumpy-surfaced eggs were 12 in (30 cm) long and had a volume of about half a gallon (2 L). At about twice the size of a modern ostrich egg, this was unusually large. The eggs were found in a crater-like nest which was arranged in a line. Did *Hypselosaurus* carefully nudge the eggs into line after laying, or did it lay its eggs while walking?

DINOSAUR

LATE CRETACEOUS

Paleontologists are still not sure what *Hypselosaurus* looked like. It was definitely small compared to other sauropods, and its legs were unusually thick. It may have had some form of armor.

NECK
The reason for its remarkably long neck is unclear, but it may have helped *Hypselosaurus* to reach plant life that others couldn't.

WHERE IN THE WORLD?

Hypselosaurus was widespread across Western Europe, in what is now Spain and France.

HOW BIG IS IT?

TEETH
Hypselosaurus had small, peg-like teeth used for cropping the plant material, but not for chewing since the jaws were not designed for it.

TIMELINE (millions of years ago)

540	505	438	408	360	280	248	208	146	65	1.8 to today

Nemegtosaurus

• **ORDER** • Saurischia • **FAMILY** • Nemegtosauridae • **GENUS & SPECIES** • *Nemegtosaurus mongoliensis*

VITAL STATISTICS

FOSSIL LOCATION	Mongolia
DIET	Herbivorous
PRONUNCIATION	NAY-meg-toe-SAWR-us
WEIGHT	Unknown
LENGTH	39 ft (12 m)
HEIGHT	Unknown
MEANING OF NAME	"Nemegt lizard" after the Nemegt Valley in Mongolia, where it was found

FOSSIL EVIDENCE

The fossil remains of other sauropods of the Late Cretaceous are often missing their skulls. The opposite is true for *Nemegtosaurus*, which is known from a partial skull and part of its neck. Its head has been compared to that of *Diplodocus*, but they were probably not related because *Diplodocus* lived during the late Jurassic Period, many millions of years earlier. Like other sauropods, *Nemegtosaurus* had peg-like teeth at the front of its jaws for stripping plant material. Its long neck allowed it to reach through the forests for foliage.

DINOSAUR

LATE CRETACEOUS

WHERE IN THE WORLD?

Nemegtosaurus was located in what is now the Gobi Desert of southern Mongolia.

Nemegtosaurus was a titanosaur, a member of the family of enormous sauropods. We don't know very much about it, but it may have had armor like its relatives. Titanosaurs, like all non-avian dinosaurs, did not survive beyond the Late Cretaceous.

BODY
If *Nemegtosaurus* did have armor, this would have been located to best protect its bulky body. Its gut was big, to process all the plant material it ate.

MOUTH
With its blunt teeth, *Nemegtosaurus* probably stripped foliage from plants and swallowed it without chewing.

HOW BIG IS IT?

TIMELINE (millions of years ago)

540	505	438	408	360	280	248	208	146	65	1.8 to today

Neuquensaurus

• ORDER • Saursichia • FAMILY • Titanosauridae • GENUS & SPECIES • *Neuquensaurus australis*

VITAL STATISTICS

Fossil Location	Argentina
Diet	Herbivorous
Pronunciation	NEH-oo-ken-SAW-rus
Weight	Unknown
Length	33–49 ft (10–15 m)
Height	Unknown
Meaning of name	"Neuquén lizard" after Neuquén Province, Argentina, where the first fossil was found

FOSSIL EVIDENCE

A titanosaurid sauropod, *Neuquensaurus* was protected by oval scutes on its back. Titanosaurs have been found on every continent except Australia, and some paleontologists believe that their armor may have been an adaptation that was important to their survival. Many sauropods had died out by the end of the Jurassic Period, perhaps because they didn't have that body armor and were vulnerable to carnivores. The titanosaurs, on the other hand, not only survived but lived all over the world, rather than being restricted (as many dinosaurs were) to certain geographic areas.

DINOSAUR

LATE CRETACEOUS

Neuquensaurus was a sauropod who lived in small herds. To have enough energy to survive, it spent much of its time eating, and possibly migrated seasonally to keep up with changes in the food supply.

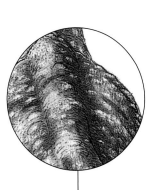

WHERE IN THE WORLD?

Neuquensaurus was located in Argentina and Uruguay, South America.

OSTEODERMS
Buried in its back were bony oval osteoderms, which offered protection against (and may even have frightened) large predators.

HOW BIG IS IT?

BODY
Neuquensaurus needed a huge gut for digesting all the plant material it ate, which was likely broken down by gastroliths (small stones) it swallowed.

TIMELINE (millions of years ago)

540	505	438	408	360	280	248	208	146	65	1.8 to today

Opisthocoelicaudia

• ORDER • Saurischia • FAMILY • Saltasauridae • GENUS & SPECIES • *Opisthocoelicaudia skarzynski*

VITAL STATISTICS

FOSSIL LOCATION	Mongolia
DIET	Herbivorous
PRONUNCIATION	Oh-PIS-tho-SEEL-ih-CAWD-ee-ah
WEIGHT	15 tons (16.5 tonnes)
LENGTH	39 ft (12 m)
HEIGHT	Unknown
MEANING OF NAME	"Hollow-backed tail" because of the opisthocoelous (hollow-behind) structure of the tail vertebrae

WHERE IN THE WORLD?

Opisthocoelicaudia was located in Mongolia, in what is now the Gobi Desert.

Most sauropods had an arched profile, but *Opisthocoelicaudia* held its body almost completely straight from its neck to its tail. It might have been able to rear up to reach leaves, resting on its legs and tail.

TAIL
Thanks to unique joints and considerable muscle attachments, the tail of *Opisthocoelicaudia* slanted upward, not downward, like other sauropods.

FOSSIL EVIDENCE

Neither the head nor neck of this creature has been found, but there are tooth marks on the pelvis and femur. This suggests scavengers fed on its body after it had died. Not far from the fossil site, the skull of *Nemegtosaurus* was found, and some paleontologists believe that the specimens are from the same dinosaur. The vertebrae of *Opisthocoelicaudia* are unique—the side facing the end of the tail cups inward; the side facing the front of the animal cups outward. This may have allowed *Opisthocoelicaudia* to use its tail as a prop.

DINOSAUR

LATE CRETACEOUS

HOW BIG IS IT?

HIND LEGS
An extra vertebra in its pelvic area and a strong hip socket might have allowed *Opisthocoelicaudia* to stand on its hind legs, unlike other sauropods.

TIMELINE (millions of years ago)

540	505	438	408	360	280	248	208	146	65	1.8 to today

Quaesitosaurus

• ORDER • Saurischia • FAMILY • Nemegtosauridae • GENUS & SPECIES • *Quaesitosaurus orientalis*

VITAL STATISTICS

FOSSIL LOCATION	Mongolia
DIET	Herbivorous
PRONUNCIATION	Kwee-SIT-oh-SAWR-us
WEIGHT	Unknown
LENGTH	Up to 75 ft (23 m)
HEIGHT	Unknown
MEANING OF NAME	"Unusual lizard" after its unusual skull

We know very little about *Quaesitosaurus*. But it is interesting to note that it and its close relative and neighbor *Nemegtosaurus* are both mainly known from skulls—usually the rarest parts of sauropods.

WHERE IN THE WORLD?

Quaesitosaurus has been located only in Mongolia.

MOUTH
Soft peg-like teeth were adapted for stripping soft plant material, which may have included plants that grew in the water. It swallowed its food whole, without chewing.

FOSSIL EVIDENCE

Quaesitosaurus is known only from a partial skull found in the Gobi Desert, a region that was semiarid during the Late Cretaceous. Large ear openings suggest that it may have had good hearing. In most cases, however, guesses about what it looked like and its behavior must be based on what is known about other sauropods. It probably traveled in herds, probably hatched from eggs, and was likely among the least intelligent of the dinosaurs. All that said, it is possible that *Quaesitosaurus* is the same as *Nemegtosaurus*.

HOW BIG IS IT?

NECK
Although no neck has been found for *Quaesitosaurus*, we know by comparison with other sauropods that it was a long one.

DINOSAUR

LATE CRETACEOUS

TIMELINE (millions of years ago)

540	505	438	408	360	280	248	208	146	65	1.8 to today

Saurolophus

• **ORDER** • Ornithischia • **FAMILY** • Hadrosauridae • **GENUS & SPECIES** • *Saurolophus osborni*

VITAL STATISTICS

FOSSIL LOCATION	Southwestern Canada, Mongolia
DIET	Herbivorous
PRONUNCIATION	SAWR-oh-LOHF-us
WEIGHT	2.6 tons (2.9 tonnes)
LENGTH	30–39 ft (9–12 m)
HEIGHT	Unknown
MEANING OF NAME	"Crested lizard" because of the small crest on top of its head

FOSSIL EVIDENCE

Some paleontologists think that *Saurolophus* had loose skin on top of its snout. It may have inflated this, either for display or to make sound. To create a loud bellow, they suggest *Saurolophus* breathed out to deflate the balloon. The air traveling through the crest and out of its nostrils made the sound, which may have been used to attract a mate or to scare a rival. Specimens have been found in Asia and North America, helping to confirm the theory that a piece of land once connected the two continents.

DINOSAUR

LATE CRETACEOUS

Saurolophus walked mostly on two legs, balanced by its tail. The top bill of its beak curved upward, and this herbivore relied on its cheek teeth to grind the twigs, seeds and conifer needles it likely ate.

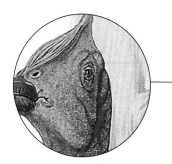

EYES
Saurolophus was one of the first hadrosaurs discovered to have a ring of bones supporting its eyes, known as a sclerotic ring.

WHERE IN THE WORLD?

Saurolophus was located on two continents—Asia and North America.

HOW BIG IS IT?

CREST
Saurolophus had a spike-like crest sticking up and back from its skull. Also found on juveniles, it was about 5 in (13 cm) long in adults.

TIMELINE (millions of years ago)

540	505	438	408	360	280	248	208	146	65	1.8 to today

Shantungosaurus

• ORDER • Ornithischia • FAMILY • Hadrosauridae • GENUS & SPECIES • *Shantungosaurus giganteus*

VITAL STATISTICS

FOSSIL LOCATION	China
DIET	Herbivorous
PRONUNCIATION	SHAHN-DUNG-oh-SAWR-us
WEIGHT	Up to 16 tons (17.6 tonnes)
LENGTH	39–49ft (12–15m)
HEIGHT	Unknown
MEANING OF NAME	"Shantung lizard" after Shantung (Shandong) province, China, where it was found

FOSSIL EVIDENCE

Shantungosaurus was discovered in 1964 and described in 1973. It is known from the incomplete remains of five individuals. All were found in the same fossil bed, their bones mixed together, suggesting that *Shantungosaurus* lived in herds. This was probably a strategy that offered some protection from tyrannosaurs, the only predators large enough to attack it. Its best defense was probably to run away, and the fossil evidence suggests it would have risen onto its powerful hind legs to do that.

DINOSAUR

LATE CRETACEOUS

A herbivore, *Shantungosaurus* had a toothless beak, but jaws that were packed with hundreds of small teeth. Foraging on coastal plains and floodplains, it was very similar to the North American *Edmontosarus*, only larger.

NOSTRILS
Around its nostrils, *Shantungosaurus* had a large hole that may have been covered by a loose skin flap, which could be inflated to make sound.

WHERE IN THE WORLD?

Shantungosaurus was located in Asia, specifically in what is now Shandong, China.

HOW BIG IS IT?

HIND LEGS
Perhaps the largest hadrosaur, *Shantungosaurus* depended on hind legs that were stout and strong to support its weight.

TIMELINE (millions of years ago)

540	505	438	408	360	280	248	208	146	65	1.8 to today

Titanosaurus

• **ORDER** • Saurischia • **FAMILY** • Titanosauridae • **GENUS & SPECIES** • *Titanosaurus indicus*

VITAL STATISTICS

Fossil Location	India
Diet	Herbivorous
Pronunciation	Tie-TAN-oh-SAWR-us
Weight	9–14 tons (9.9–15.4 tonnes)
Length	39–59 ft (12–18 m)
Height	Unknown
Meaning of name	"Titanic lizard" because of the size of the vertebrae

WHERE IN THE WORLD?

Specimens thought to be *Titanosaurus* have been found in Argentina and Hungary, but the only true specimens are from India.

One of the last of the giant sauropods to roam the Earth, *Titanosaurus* was protected by bony plates across its back.

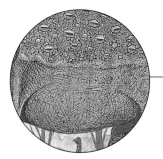

BODY
Titanosaurus's huge gut probably contained gastroliths (small stones) to help it digest the large amounts of vegetation it ate.

FOSSIL EVIDENCE

Titanosaurus was found in India in 1870, when limb bones and a few vertebrae were discovered. For years afterward, *Titanosaurus* was a "wastebin taxon," which is a species to which specimens are assigned because they have features that fit nowhere else. However, later discoveries have shown that these features are not unique and do actually belong to related dinosaurs that we already know about. What this means is that *Titanosaurus* is now considered by most scientists a *nomen dubium* (Latin for "dubious name") as its features cannot be distinguished from other dinosaurs.

TAIL
It is unlikely that *Titanosaurus* used its long tail in defense; it was simply a counterbalance to its long neck.

HOW BIG IS IT?

DINOSAUR

LATE CRETACEOUS

TIMELINE (millions of years ago)

540	505	438	408	360	280	248	208	146	65	1.8 to today

Lambeosaurus

• ORDER • Ornithischia •
• FAMILY • Hadrosauridae • GENUS & SPECIES • Several species within the genus *Lambeosaurus*

VITAL STATISTICS

FOSSIL LOCATION	North America
DIET	Herbivorous
PRONUNCIATION	Lam-bee-oh-SAWR-us
WEIGHT	Up to 25 tons (23 tonnes)
LENGTH	30–50 ft (9–15 m)
HEIGHT	7 ft (2.1 m) at the hips
MEANING OF NAME	"Lambe's lizard" after Canadian fossil hunter Charles Lambe

FOSSIL EVIDENCE

More than 20 fossils have been found and a number of species named, some of which may simply be juveniles rather than new, small species. This variety has led to very different estimates of *Lambeosaurus'* typical size. All of the *Lambeosaurus* species had crests. One was shaped like a hatchet buried in the skull; another was a single ridge. The purpose of these crests is unknown. Their hollow structure may have added volume to the animal's cries. Instead, they may have been for ritual display or maybe to tell the difference between males and females.

DINOSAUR

LATE CRETACEOUS

Lambeosaurus was one of the largest of the duck-billed dinosaurs and had a head crest that varied between species. Paleontologists still aren't sure what the crest was for. Was it for display, to make sounds, or for picking up scent?

TEETH
There may have been as many as 1600 tightly wedged teeth in *Lambeosaurus'* mouth, so the ones broken by constant chewing were immediately replaced.

WHERE IN THE WORLD?

Fossils show that Lambeosaurus lived in Alberta, Canada, and in Montana and New Mexico.

LEGS AND TAIL
Lambeosaurus could move on four legs (to forage) or possibly two legs (to run). Its tail was stiffened with tendons to prevent it from drooping.

HOW BIG IS IT?

TIMELINE (millions of years ago)

540	505	438	408	360	280	248	208	146	65	1.8 to today

Saltasaurus

• ORDER • Saurischia • FAMILY • Saltasauridae • GENUS & SPECIES • *Saltasaurus loricatu*

VITAL STATISTICS

FOSSIL LOCATION	Argentina
DIET	Herbivorous
PRONUNCIATION	Salta-SAWR-us
WEIGHT	7 tons (6.3 tonnes)
LENGTH	40 ft (12 m)
HEIGHT	16 ft (5 m)
MEANING OF NAME	"Salta lizard" after Salta Province, Argentina, where it was found

FOSSIL EVIDENCE

Saltasaurus was found in 1980. Although it has been discovered in only one place so far, there are a good number of fossils for paleontologists to study. At Salta Province in northwest Argentina, scientists have found several of the egg-shaped or circular armored plates that once covered *Saltasaurus*' back and may have protected it from attack by predators. Hundreds of 0.25 in (6.7 mm) bumps grew on the plates. Several partial skeletons found have included vertebrae, leg bones and jawbones.

Like many plant-eating dinosaurs, *Saltasaurus* had a very large body and a small head and long neck so it could stretch up to reach leaves or fruits on high branches.

ARMOR
Saltasaurus was well protected by its armor, which covered its back and tail and extended up its neck.

Saltasaurus was found in northwest Argentina in South America, in the area around Salta Province.

EGGS
Saltasaurus was a very big dinosaur, but eggs of its close relatives found in 1997 in Patagonia, Argentina, were only around 4 in (12 cm) long.

HOW BIG IS IT?

DINOSAUR

LATE CRETACEOUS

TIMELINE (millions of years ago)

540	505	438	408	360	280	248	208	146	65	1.8 to today

Glossary

arteries (AR-tuh-rees) Vessels that carry blood from the heart to the rest of the body

basal (BAY-sil) Foundation, starting at the very base, or bottom

cartilage (KAR-dih-lij) An elastic tissue found in joints and respiratory passages

floodplain (FLUD-playn) A flat area of land that is occasionally submerged in floodwater

fossil (FAH-sil) Remains or traces of an organism from the past that have been preserved, such as bones, teeth, footprints, etc.

gizzard (GIH-zerd) An organ found in some animals, made of thick muscle. Acts as a second stomach where food is ground up, then passed to the true stomach

herd (HURD) A group of animals of the same kind

hexagon (HEK-suh-gon) A shape with six sides

isthmus (IHS-mus) A narrow strip of land that connects two larger land areas

migrate (MY-grait) To move from one place to another

quadrupedal (kwah-DRU-pih-dul) An animal with four feet

spatulate (SPAT-chu-lit) Shaped like a spatula, a thin kitchen tool used for spreading soft substances, like cake frosting

trod (TRAWD) Walked

tubercles (TU-ber-kulz) Small bumps on the skin of a plant or animal

Index

A

Aeolosaurus..........31
Africa..........18-19
Alamosaurus..........32
Allosaurus..........15, 18
Amargasaurus..........26-29
Antarctosaurus..........33
Apatosaurus..........21, 24
Argentina..........26-27, 29-31, 33, 37, 42, 44
Argentinosaurus..........30
Asia..........40-41
Australia..........6, 29, 37

B

bone wars..........24
Bothriospondylus..........10
Brachiosaurus..........15, 18-21
Brontosaurus..........24
Browne, Arthur..........6

C

Camarasaurus..........24
Canada..........34, 40, 43
cartilage..........6
Ceratosaurus..........15
Cetiosauriscus..........9
Cetiosaurus..........8-9
China..........7, 13, 41
Colorado..........14-15, 19
conifers..........14, 34, 40
Cope, Edward..........24
Cretaceous Period..........25
cycads..........14, 21

D

Dacentrurus..........16-17
Dicraeosaurus..........11
Diplodocus..........9, 12, 21-22, 29-30, 36
Dryosaurus..........21

E

Edmontosaurus..........34, 41
elephants..........6
England..........8-10, 16, 25
Euhelopus..........13
Europe..........16, 18-19, 25, 35

F

femur..........6, 17, 38
fossil triangle..........6
France..........16, 35

G

Gargantuavis..........35
gastralia..........12
gastroliths..........5, 9-10, 22-23, 32-33, 37, 42
gigantotherms..........21
giraffe..........15, 18
gizzard..........9-10, 18, 22, 32
Gobi Desert..........36, 38-39

H

hadrosaurs..........40-41
Haplocanthosaurus..........14
Hungary..........42
Hypselosaurus..........35

I

Iguanodon..........25
India..........33, 42
Isle of Wight..........8, 25

J

Jurassic Period..........6-24, 36-37

L

Lambe, Charles..........43
Lambeosaurus..........43
lizard..........5-9, 11, 14-15, 24-26, 30-37, 39-44

M

Madagascar..........10
Marsh, Othniel..........24
Melanorosaurus..........5
Mexico..........24
Mongolia..........36, 38-40
Montana..........43
Morrison Formation..........12, 14
mosasaurs..........24

N

Nemegtosaurus..........36, 39
Neuquensaurus..........37
New Mexico..........23, 32, 43
North America..........14, 32, 34, 40, 43

O

Omasaurus..........16
Omeisaurus..........7
Opisthocoelicaudia..........38
osteoderms..........30, 37
ostrich..........35

P

paleontologist..........7, 17, 19, 21, 35, 37-38, 40, 43-44
Panama..........32
Patagonia..........27, 44
Pelorosaurus..........25
Portugal..........16, 35
prosauropods..........5

Q

Quaesitosaurus..........39

R

reptile..........8, 18, 22, 23
Rhoetosaurus..........6

S

sacral vertebrae..........5
Saltasaurus..........44
Saurolophus..........40
sauropod..........5-9, 11-15, 24, 26, 31-33, 35-39, 42
Seismosaurus..........22-23
Shantungosaurus..........41
Shunosaurus..........7
South Africa..........5
South America..........30, 32-33, 37, 44
Spain..........16, 35
stegosaur..........16
stegosaurid..........17
Stegosaurus..........16-17, 21

T

Taihang Mountains..........13
Tanzania..........10-11
Texas..........32
theropods..........32
titanosaur..........30, 36-37
Titanosaurus..........42
Triassic Period..........5
tyrannosaurs..........32, 41
Tyrannosaurus rex..........34

U

Ultrasauros..........15
Uruguay..........37
Utah..........32

W

whale..........8-9
World War II..........16
Wyoming..........12, 24

For More Information

Books

Gray, Susan Heinrichs. *Apatosaurus.* Mankato, MN: Child's World, 2004.

Kimmel, Elizabeth Cody. *Dinosaur Bone War: Cope and Marsh's Fossil Feud.* New York: Random House, 2006.

Malam, John. *Dinosaur Atlas: An Amazing Journey Through a Lost World.* New York: DK Publishing, 2006.

Web Sites

To ensure the currency and safety of recommended Internet links, Windmill maintains and updates an online list of sites related to the subject of this book. To access this list of Web sites, please go to www.windmillbooks.com/weblinks and select this book's title.

For more great fiction and nonfiction, go to www.windmillbooks.com.